What Men Live By

Tolstoi

COPYRIGHT, 1888, BY
THOMAS Y. CROWELL & CO.

PRESS OF
Rockwell and Churchill,
BOSTON.

WHAT MEN LIVE BY.

We know that we have passed out of death into life, because we love the brethren. He that loveth not abideth in death. (I. Epistle of St. John, iii. 14.)

But whoso hath the world's goods, and beholdeth his brother in need, and shutteth up his compassion from him, how doth the love of God abide in him?

My little children, let us not love in word, neither with the tongue, but in deed and truth. (iii. 17, 18.)

Love is of God; and every one that loveth is begotten of God and knoweth God.

He that loveth not knoweth not God; for God is love. (iv. 7, 8.)

No man hath beheld God at any time: if we love one another, God abideth in us. (iv. 12.)

God is love; and he that abideth in love abideth in God, and God abideth in him. (iv. 16.)

If a man say, I love God, and hateth his brother, he is a liar: for he that loveth not his brother whom he hath seen cannot love God whom he hath not seen. (iv. 20.)

I.

A COBBLER and his wife and children had lodgings with a peasant. He owned neither house nor land, and he supported himself and his family by shoemaking.

Bread was dear and labor poorly paid, and whatever he earned went for food.

WHAT MEN LIVE BY.

The cobbler and his wife had one shuba*
between them, and this had come to tatters,
and for two years the cobbler had been hoarding in order to buy skeepskins for a new
shuba.

When autumn came, the cobbler's hoard had
grown; three paper rubles† lay in his wife's
box, and five rubles and twenty kopeks more
were due the cobbler from his customers.

One morning the cobbler betook himself to
the village to get his new shuba. He put on
his wife's wadded nankeen jacket over his
shirt, and outside of all a woollen kaftan.
He put the three ruble notes in his pocket,
broke off a staff, and after breakfast he set
forth.

He said to himself, "I will get my five
rubles from the peasant, and that with these
three will buy pelts for my shuba."

The cobbler reached the village and went
to one peasant's; he was not at home, but his
wife promised to send her husband with the

---

* Fur or sheepskin outside garment.

† The paper ruble is worth about forty-two cents; a ruble contains 100 kopeks.

money the next week, but she could not give him any money. He went to another, and this peasant swore that he had no money at all; but he paid him twenty kopeks for cobbling his boots.

The cobbler made up his mind to get the pelts on credit. But the fur-dealer refused to sell on credit. "Bring the money," says he; "then you can make your choice: but we know how hard it is to get what is one's due."

And so the cobbler did not do his errand, but he had the twenty kopeks for cobbling the boots, and he took from a peasant an old pair of felt boots to mend with leather.

At first the cobbler was vexed at heart; then he spent the twenty kopeks for vodka, and started to go home. In the morning he had felt cold, but after having drunken the vodka he was warm enough even without the shuba.

The cobbler was walking along the road, striking the frozen ground with the staff that he had in one hand, and swinging the felt boots in the other, and thus he talked to himself:—

"I," says he, "am warm even without a

shuba. I drank a glass, and it dances through all my veins. And so I don't need a sheepskin coat. I walk along, and all my vexation is forgotten. That is just like me! What do I need? I can get along without the shuba. I don't need it at all. There's one thing: the wife will feel bad. Indeed, it is too bad; here I have been working for it, and now to have missed it! You just wait now! if you don't bring the money, I will take your hat, I vow I will! What a way of doing things! He pays me twenty kopeks at a time! Now what can you do with twenty kopeks? Get a drink; that's all! You say, 'I am poor!' But if you are poor, how is it with me? You have a house and cattle and everything; I have nothing but my own hands. You raise your own grain, but I have to buy mine, when I can, and it costs me three rubles a week for food alone. When I get home now, we shall be out of bread. Another ruble and a half of out-go! So you must give me what you owe me."

By this time the cobbler had reached the chapel at the cross-roads, and he saw something white behind the chapel.

WHAT MEN LIVE BY.

It was already twilight, and the cobbler strained his eyes, but he could not make out what the object was.

"There never was any such stone there," he said to himself. "A cow? But it does not look like a cow! The head is like a man's; but what is that white? And why should there be any man there?"

He went nearer. Now he could see plainly. What a strange thing! It is indeed a man, but is he alive or dead? sitting there stark naked, leaning against the chapel, and not moving.

The cobbler was frightened. He thinks to himself: "Some one has killed that man, stripped him, and flung him down there. If I go near, I may get into trouble."

And the cobbler hurried by.

In passing the chapel he could no longer see the man; but after he was fairly beyond it, he looked back, and saw that the man was no longer leaning against the chapel, but was moving, and apparently looking after him.

The cobbler was still more scared by this, and he thinks to himself: "Shall I go to him or go on? If I go to him, there might something unpleasant happen; who knows what sort of a man he is? He can't have gone there for any good purpose? If I went to him, he might spring on me and choke me, and I could not get away from him; and even if he did not choke me, why should I try to make his acquaintance? What could be done with him, naked as he is? I can't take him with me, and give him my own clothes! That would be absurd"

And the cobbler hastened his steps. He had already gone some distance beyond the chapel, when his conscience began to prick him.

He stopped short.

"What is this that you are doing, Semyón?" he asked himself. "A man is perishing of cold, and you are frightened, and hurry by! Are you so very rich? Are you afraid of losing your money? Aï, Sema! That is not right!"

Semyón turned and went to the man.

II.

Semyón went back to the man, looked at him, and saw that it was a young man in the prime of life; there are no bruises visible on him, but he is evidently freezing and afraid; he is sitting there, leaning back, and does not look at Semyón; apparently he is so weak that he cannot lift his eyes.

Semyón went up close to him, and suddenly the man seemed to revive; he lifted his head and fastened his eyes on Semyón.

And by this glance the man won Semyón's heart.

He threw the felt boots down on the ground, took off his belt and laid it on the boots, and pulled off his kaftan.

"There's nothing to be said," he exclaimed. "Put these on! There now!"

Semyón put his hand under the man's elbow, to help him, and tried to lift him. The man got up.

And Semyón sees that his body is graceful and clean, that his hands and feet are comely, and that his face is agreeable. Semyón threw the kaftan over his shoulders. He could not get his arms into the sleeves. Semyón found the place for him, pulled the coat up, wrapped it around him, and fastened the belt.

He took off his tattered cap, and was going to give it to the stranger, but his head felt cold, and he thinks: "The whole top of my head is bald, but he has long curly hair."

So he put his hat on again. "I had better let him put on my boots."

He made him sit down and put on the felt boots.

After the cobbler had thus dressed him, he says: "There now, brother, just stir about, and you will get warmed up. All these things are in other hands than ours. Can you walk?"

The man stands up, looks affectionately at Semyón, but is unable to speak a word.

"Why don't you say something? We can't spend the winter here. We must get to shelter. Now, then, lean on my stick, if you don't feel strong enough. Bestir yourself!"

And the man started to move. And he walked easily, and did not lag behind. As they walked along the road Semyón said: "Where are you from, if I may ask?"

"I do not belong hereabouts."

"No; I know all the people of this region.

How did you happen to come here and get to that chapel?"

"I cannot tell you."

"Some one must have treated you outrageously?"

"No one has treated me outrageously. God has punished me."

"God does all things, but you must have been on the road to somewhere? Where do you want to go?"

"It makes no difference to me."

Semyón was surprised. The man did not look like a malefactor, and his speech was gentle, but he seemed reticent about himself.

And Semyón says to himself, "Such things as this do not happen every day." And he says to the man, "Well, come to my house, though you will find it very narrow quarters."

As Semyón approached the yard, the stranger did not lag behind, but walked abreast of him. The wind had arisen, and searched under Semyón's shirt, and as the effect of the wine had now passed away, he began to be chilled to the bone. He walked along, and began to snuffle, and he muffled his wife's jacket closer around him, and he thinks: "That's the way you get a shuba! You go after a shuba, and you come home without your kaftan! yes, and you bring with you a naked man—besides, Matrióna won't take kindly to it!"

And as soon as the thought of Matrióna occurred to him, he began to feel downhearted.

But as soon as his eyes fell on the stranger, he remembered what a look he had given him behind the chapel, and his heart danced with joy.

III.

Semyón's wife finished her work early. She had chopped wood, brought water, fed the children, taken her own supper, and was now deliberating when it would be best to mix some bread, "to-day or to-morrow?"

A large crust was still left. She thinks: "If Semyón gets something to eat in town, he won't care for much supper, and the bread will last till to-morrow."

Matrióna contemplated the crust for some time, and said to herself: "I am not going to mix any bread. There's just enough flour to make one more loaf. We shall get along till Friday."

Matrióna put away the bread, and sat down at the table to sew a patch on her husband's shirt.

She sews, and thinks how her husband will be buying pelts for the shuba.

"I hope the fur-dealer will not cheat him. For he is as simple as he can be. He, himself, would not cheat anybody, but a baby could lead him by the nose. Eight rubles is no small sum. You can get a fine shuba with it. Perhaps not one tanned, but still a good one. How we suffered last winter without any shuba! Could not go to the river nor anywhere! And whenever he went out-doors, he put on all the clothes, and I hadn't anything to wear. He is late in getting home. He ought to be here by this time. I hope my sweetheart has not got drunk."

Just as these thoughts were passing through her mind the doorsteps creaked; some one was at the door. Matrióna stuck in the needle, went to the entry. There she sees that two men had come in, — Semyón, and with him a strange peasant, without a cap and in felt boots.

Matrióna perceived immediately that her husband's breath smelt of wine. "Now," she thinks, "he has gone and got drunk."

And when she saw that he had not his kaftan on, and wore only her jacket, and had nothing in his hands, and said nothing, but only simpered, Matrióna's heart failed within her.

"He has drunk up the money, he has been on a spree with this miserable beggar; and, worse than all, he has gone and brought him home!"

Matrióna let them pass by her into the cottage; then she herself went in: she saw that the stranger was young, and that he had on their kaftan. There was no shirt to be seen under the kaftan; and he wore no cap.

As soon as he went in, he paused, and did not move and did not raise his eyes.

And Matrióna thinks: "He is not a good man; his conscience troubles him."

Matrióna scowled, went to the oven, and watched to see what they would do.

Semyón took off his cap and sat down on the

bench good-naturedly. "Well," says he, "Matrióna, can't you get us something to eat?"

Matrióna muttered something under her breath.

She did not offer to move, but as she stood by the oven she looked from one to the other and kept shaking her head.

Semyón saw that his wife was out of sorts and would not do anything, but he pretended not to notice it and took the stranger by the arm.

"Sit down, brother," says he; "we'll have some supper."

The stranger sat down on the bench.

"Well," says Semyón, "haven't you cooked anything?"

Matrióna's anger blazed out. "I cooked," says she, "but not for you. You are a fine man! I see you have been drinking! You went to get a shuba, and you have come home without your kaftan. And, then, you have brought home this naked vagabond with you. I haven't any supper for such drunkards as you are!"

"That'll do, Matrióna; what is the use of

letting your tongue run on so? If you had only asked first: 'What kind of a man...'"

"You just tell me what you have done with the money!"

Semyón went to his kaftan, took out the bills, spread them out on the table.

"Here's the money, but Trífonof did not pay me; he promised it to-morrow."

Matrióna grew still more angry.

"You didn't buy the new shuba, and you have given away your only kaftan to this naked vagabond whom you have brought home!"

She snatched the money from the table, and went off to hide it away, saying:—

"I haven't any supper. I can't feed all your drunken beggars!"

"Hey there! Matrióna, just hold your tongue! First you listen to what I have to say..."

"Much sense should I hear from a drunken fool! Good reason I had for not wanting to marry such a drunkard as you are. Mother gave me linen, and you have wasted it in drink; you went to get a shuba, and you spent it for drink."

Semyón was going to assure his wife that he

had spent only twenty kopeks for drink; he was going to tell her where he had found the man, but Matrióna would not give him a chance to speak a word; it was perfectly marvellous, but she managed to speak two words at once! Things that had taken place ten years before — she called them all up.

Matrióna scolded and scolded; then she sprang at Semyón and seized him by the sleeve.

"Give me back my jacket! It's the only one I have, and you took it from me and put it on yourself. Give it here, you miserable dog! bestir yourself, you villain!"

Semyón began to strip off the jacket. As he was pulling his arms out of the sleeves, his wife gave it a twitch and split the jacket up the seams. Matrióna snatched the garment away, threw it over her head, and started for the door. She intended to go out, but she paused, and her heart was pulled in two directions, — she wanted to vent her spite, and she wanted to find what kind of a man the stranger was.

IV.

Matrióna paused, and said:—

"If he were a good man, then he would not have been naked; why, even now, he hasn't any shirt on; if he had been engaged in decent business, you would have told where you discovered such an elegant fellow!"

"Well, I was going to tell you. I was walking along, and there behind the chapel, this man was sitting, stark naked, and half frozen to death. It is not summer, mind you, for a naked man! God brought me to him, else he would have perished. Now what could I do? Such things don't happen every day. I took and dressed him, and brought him home with me. Calm your anger. It's a sin, Matrióna; we must all die."

Matrióna was about to make a surly reply, but her eyes fell on the stranger, and she held her peace.

The stranger was sitting motionless on the edge of the bench, just as he had sat down. His hands were folded on his knees, his head was bent on his breast, his eyes were shut, and he kept frowning, as though something stifled him.

Matrióna made no reply.

Semyón went on to say, "Matrióna, can it be that God is not in you?"

Matrióna heard his words, and glanced again at the stranger, and suddenly her anger vanished. She turned from the door, went to the corner where the oven was, and brought the supper.

She set a bowl on the table, poured out the kvas,* and put on the last of the crust. She gave them the knife and the spoons.

"Have some victuals," she said.

Semyón touched the stranger. "Draw up, young man," says he.

Semyón cut the bread, crumbled it into the bowl, and they began to eat their supper. And Matrióna sat at the end of the table, leaned on her hand, and gazed at the stranger. And Matrióna began to feel sorry for him, and she conceived affection for him.

And suddenly the stranger brightened up,

* Fermented drink made of rye meal or soaked bread crumbs.

ceased to frown, lifted his eyes to Matrióna and smiled.

After they had finished their supper, the woman cleared off the things, and began to question the stranger: —

"Where are you from?"

"I do not belong hereabouts."

"How did you happen to get into this road?"

"I cannot tell you."

"Who maltreated you?"

"God punished me."

"And you were lying there stripped?"

"Yes; there I was lying all naked, freezing to death, when Semyón saw me, had compassion on me, took off his kaftan, put it on me, and bade me come home with him. And here you have fed me, given me something to eat and to drink, and have taken pity on me. May the Lord requite you!"

Matrióna got up, took from the window Semyón's old shirt which she had been patching, and gave it to the stranger; then she found a pair of drawers and gave them also to him.

"There now," says she, "I see that you have no shirt. Put these things on, and then lie down wherever you please, in the loft or on the oven."

The stranger took off the kaftan, put on the shirt, and went to bed in the loft. Matrióna put out the light, took the kaftan, and lay down beside her husband.

Matrióna covered herself up with the skirt of the kaftan, but she lay without sleeping: she could not get the thought of the stranger out of her mind.

When she remembered that he had eaten her last crust, and that there was no bread for the morrow, when she remembered that she had given him the shirt and the drawers, she felt disturbed; but then came the thought of how he had smiled at her, and her heart leaped within her.

Matrióna lay long without falling asleep, and when she heard that Semyón was also awake, she pulled up the kaftan, and said: —

"Semyón!"

"Ha?"

"You ate up the last of the bread, and I

did not mix any more. I don't know how we shall get along to-morrow. Perhaps I might borrow some of neighbor Malánya."

"We shall get along; we shall have enough."

The wife lay without speaking. Then she said:—

"Well, he seems like a good man; but why doesn't he tell us about himself?"

"It must be because he can't."

"Sióm!"*

"Ha?"

"We are always giving; why doesn't some one give to us?"

Semyón did not know what reply to make. Saying, "You have talked enough!" he turned over and went to sleep.

V.

In the morning Semyón woke up.

His children were still asleep; his wife had gone to a neighbor's to get some bread. The stranger of the evening before, dressed in the old shirt and drawers, was sitting alone on the bench, looking up. And his face was brighter

* Diminutive of Semyón, or Simon.

than it had been the evening before. And Semyón said:—

"Well, my dear, the belly asks for bread, and the naked body for clothes. You must earn your own living. What do you know how to do?"

"There is nothing that I know how to do."

Semyón was amazed, and he said:—

"If one has only the mind to, men can learn anything."

"Men work, and I will work."

"What is your name?"

"Mikháïla."

"Well, Mikháïla, if you aren't willing to tell about yourself, that is your affair; but you must earn your own living. If you will work as I shall show you, I will keep you."

"The Lord requite you! I am willing to learn; only show me what to do."

Semyón took a thread, drew it through his fingers, and showed him how to make a waxed end.

"It does not take much skill — look ..."

Mikháïla looked, also twisted the thread between his fingers: he instantly imitated him, and finished the point.

Semyón showed him how to make the welt. This also Mikháila immediately understood. The shoemaker likewise showed him how to twist the bristle into the thread, and how to use the awl; and these things also Mikháila immeately learned to do.

Whatever part of the work Semyón showed him he imitated him in, and in two days he was able to work as though he had been all his life a cobbler. He worked without relaxation, he ate little, and when his work was done he would sit silent, looking up. He did not go on the street, he spoke no more than was absolutely necessary, he never jested, he never laughed.

The only time that he was seen to smile was on the first evening when the woman got him his supper.

VI.

Day after day, week after week rolled by for a whole year.

Mikháila lived on in the same way, working for Semyón. And the fame of Semyón's apprentice went abroad; no one, it was said, could make such neat, strong boots as Semyón's apprentice Mikháïla. And from all around people came to Semyón to have boots made, and Semyón began to lay up money.

One winter's day, as Semyón and Mikháïla were sitting at their work, a sleigh drawn by a troïka drove up to the cottage, with a jingling of bells.

They looked out of the window: the sleigh stopped in front of the cottage; a footman jumped down from the box and opened the door. A bárin * in a fur coat got out of the sleigh, walked up to Semyón's cottage, and mounted the steps. Matrióna hurried to throw the door wide open.

The bárin bent his head and entered the cottage; when he drew himself up to his full height, his head almost touched the ceiling; he seemed to take up nearly all the room.

Semyón rose and bowed; he was surprised to see the bárin. He had never before seen such a man.

Semyón himself was thin, the stranger was spare, and Matrióna was like a dry twig; but this man seemed to be from a different world.

* The ordinary title of any landowner or noble.

His face was ruddy and full, his neck was like a bull's; it seemed as though he were made out of cast iron.

The bárin got his breath, took off his shuba, sat down on the bench, and said: —

"Which is the master-shoemaker?"

Semyón stepped out. Says he, "I, your Honor."

The bárin shouted to his footman: "Hey, Fedka,* bring me the leather."

The young fellow ran out and brought back a parcel. The bárin took the parcel and laid it on the table.

"Open it," said he. The footman opened it.

The bárin touched the leather with his finger, and said to Semyón: —

"Now listen, shoemaker. Do you see this leather?"

"I see it, your Honor," says he.

"Well, do you appreciate what kind of leather it is?"

Semyón felt of the leather, and said, "Fine leather."

"Indeed it's fine! Fool that you are! you

* Diminutive of Feódor, Theodore.

never in your life saw such before! German leather. It cost twenty rubles."

Semyón was startled. He said: —

"Where, indeed, could we have seen anything like it?"

"Well, that's all right. Can you make from this leather a pair of boots that will fit me?"

"I can, your Honor."

The bárin shouted at him: —

"'Can' is a good word. Now just realize whom you are making those boots for, and out of what kind of leather. You must make a pair of boots, so that when the year is gone they won't have got out of shape, or ripped. If you can, then take the job and cut the leather; but if you can't, then don't take it and don't cut the leather. I will tell you beforehand, if the boots rip or wear out of shape before the year is out, I will have you locked up; but if they don't rip or get out of shape before the end of the year, then I will give you ten rubles for your work."

Semyón was frightened, and was at a loss what to say.

He glanced at Mikháïla. He nudged him

with his elbow, and whispered, "Had I better take it?"

Mikháila nodded his head, meaning, "You had better take the job."

Semyón took Mikháila's advice: he agreed to make a pair of boots that would not rip or wear out of shape before the year was over.

The bárin shouted to his footman, ordered him to take the boot from his left foot; then he stretched out his leg.

"Take the measure!"

Semyón cut off a piece of paper seventeen inches * long, smoothed it out, knelt down, wiped his hands nicely on his apron so as not to soil the bárin's stockings, and began to take the measure.

Semyón took the measure of the sole, he took the measure of the instep; then he started to measure the calf of the leg, but the paper was not long enough. The leg at the calf was as thick as a beam.

"Look out; don't make it too tight around the calf!"

Semyón was going to cut another piece of

* Ten vershóks, equivalent to 17.50 inches.

paper. The bárin sat there, rubbing his toes together in his stockings, and looking at the inmates of the cottage: he caught sight of Mikháila.

"Who is that yonder?" he demanded; "does he belong to you?"

"He is my workman. He will make the boots."

"Look here," says the bárin to Mikháila, "remember that they are to be made so as to last a whole year."

Semyón also looked at Mikháila; he saw that Mikháila was paying no attention, but was standing in the corner, as though he saw some one there behind the bárin. Mikháila gazed and gazed, and suddenly smiled, and his whole face lighted up.

"What a fool you are, showing your teeth that way! You had better see to it that the boots are ready in time."

And Mikháila replied, "They will be ready as soon as they are needed."

"Very well."

The bárin drew on his boot, buttoned up his shuba, and went to the door. But he forgot to stoop, and so struck his head against the lintel.

The bárin stormed and rubbed his head; then he climbed into his sleigh and drove off. After the bárin was gone Semyón said:—

"Well, he's as solid as a rock! You could not kill him with a mallet. His head almost broke the door-post, but it did not seem to hurt him much."

And Matrióna said: "How can they help getting fat, living as they do? Even death does not carry off such a nail as he is."

And Semyón says to Mikhaíla: "Now, you see, we have taken this work, and we must do it as well as we can. The leather is costly, and the bárin gruff. We must not make any blunder. Now, your eye has become quicker, and your hand is more skilful than mine; there's the measure. Cut out the leather, and I will be finishing up those vamps."

Mikhaíla did not fail to do as he was told; he took the bárin's leather, stretched it out on the table, doubled it over, took the knife, and began to cut.

Matrióna came and watched Mikhaíla as he

cut, and she was amazed to see what he was doing. For she was used to cobbler's work, and she looks and sees that Mikhaïla is not cutting the leather for boots, but in rounded fashion.

Matrióna wanted to speak, but she thought in her own mind: "Of course I can't be expected to understand how to make boots for gentlemen; Mikhaïla must understand it better than I do; I will not interfere."

After he had cut out the work, he took his waxed ends and began to sew, not as one does in making boots, with double threads, but with one thread, just as slippers are made.

Matrióna wondered at this also, but still she did not like to interfere. And Mikhaïla kept on steadily with his work.

It came time for the nooning; Semyón got up, looked, and saw that Mikhaïla had been making slippers out of the bárin's leather. Semyón groaned.

"How is this?" he asks himself. "Mikhaïla has lived with me a whole year, and never made a mistake, and now he has made such a blunder! The bárin ordered thick-soled boots, and he has been making slippers without soles! He has ruined the leather. How can I make it right with the bárin? You can't find such leather."

And he said to Mikháila:—

"What is this you have been doing?... My dear fellow, you have ruined me! You know the bárin ordered boots, and what have you made?"

He was right in the midst of his talk with Mikháila when a knock came at the rapper; some one was at the door. They looked out of the window; some one had come on horseback, and was fastening the horse. They opened the door. The same bárin's footman came walking in.

"Good day."

"Good day to you; what is it?"

"My mistress sent me in regard to a pair of boots."

"What about the boots?"

"It is this. My bárin does not need the boots; he isn't alive any more."

"What is that you say?"

"He did not live to get home from your

house; he died in the sleigh. When the sleigh reached home, we went to help him out, but there he had fallen over like a bag, and there he lay stone-dead, and it took all our strength to lift him out of the sleigh. And his lady has sent me, saying: 'Tell the shoemaker of whom your bárin just ordered boots from leather which he left with him — tell him that the boots are not needed, and that he is to make a pair of slippers for the corpse out of that leather just as quick as possible.' And I was to wait till they were made, and take them home with me. And so I have come."

Mikháïla took the rest of the leather from the table and rolled it up; he also took the slippers, which were all done, slapped them together, wiped them with his apron, and gave them to the young man. The young man took them.

"Good by, friends! Good luck to you!"

VII.

Still another year, and then two more passed by, and Mikháïla had now been living five years with Semyón. He lived in just the same way as before. He never went anywhere, he kept his own counsels, and in all that time he smiled only twice, — once when Matrióna gave him something to eat; and the other time when he smiled on the bárin.

Semyón was more than contented with his apprentice, and he no longer asked him where he came from; his only fear was lest he should leave him.

One time they were all at home. The mother was putting the iron kettles on the oven, and the children were playing on the benches and looking out of the window. Semyón was pegging away at one window, and Mikháila at the other was putting lifts on a heel.

One of the boys ran along the bench toward Mikháila, leaned over his shoulder, and looked out of the window.

"Uncle Mikháila, just look! a merchant's wife is coming to our house with some little girls. And one of the little girls is a cripple."

The words were scarcely out of the boy's mouth before Mikháila threw down his work, leaned over toward the window, and looked out of doors. And Semyón was surprised.

WHAT MEN LIVE BY.

Never before had Mikháïla cared to look out, but now his face seemed soldered to the window; he was looking at something very intently.

Semyón also looked out of the window: he sees a woman coming straight through his yard; she is neatly dressed; she has two little girls by the hand; they wear shubkas,* and kerchiefs over their heads. The little girls looked so much alike that it was hard to tell them apart, except that one of the little girls was lame in her foot: she limped as she walked.

The woman came into the entry, felt about in the dark, lifted the latch, and opened the door. She let the two little girls go before her into the cottage, and then she followed.

"How do you do, friends?"

"Welcome! What can we do for you?"

The woman sat down by the table; the two little girls clung to her knee: they were bashful.

"These little girls need to have some goatskin shoes made for the spring."

"Well, it can be done. We don't generally

* Little fur garments.

make such small ones; but it's perfectly easy, either with welts or lined with linen. This here is Mikháïla; he's my workman."

Semyón glanced at Mikháïla, and sees that he has thrown down his work, and is sitting with his eyes fastened on the little girls.

And Semyón was amazed at Mikháïla. To be sure the little girls were pretty: they had dark eyes, they were plump and rosy, and they wore handsome shubkas and kerchiefs; but still Semyón cannot understand why he gazes so intently at them, as though they were friends of his.

Semyón was amazed, and got up, and began to talk with the woman, and to make his bargain. After he had made his bargain, he began to take the measures. The woman lifted on her lap the little cripple, and said: "Take two measures from this one; make one little shoe from the twisted foot, and three from the well one. Their feet are alike; they are twins."

Semyón took his tape, and said in reference to the little cripple: "How did this happen to her? She is such a pretty little girl. Was she born so?"

"No; her mother crushed it."

Matrióna joined the conversation; she was anxious to learn who the woman and children were, and so she said:—

"Then you aren't their mother?"

"No; I am not their mother; I am no relation to them, good wife, and they are no relation to me at all: I adopted them."

"If they are not your children, you take good care of them."

"Why shouldn't I take good care of them? I nursed them both at my own breast. I had a baby of my own, but God took him. I did not take such good care of him as I do of these."

"Whose children are they?"

VIII.

The woman became confidential, and began to tell them about it.

"Six years ago," said she, "these little ones were left orphans in one week: the father was buried on Tuesday, and the mother died on Friday. Three days these little ones remained without their father, and then their mother followed him. At that time I was living with my husband in the country: we were neighbors; we lived on adjoining farms. Their father was a peasant, and worked in the forest at wood-cutting. And they were felling a tree, and it caught him across the body. It hurt him all inside. As soon as they got him out, he gave his soul to God, and that same week his wife gave birth to twins — these are the little girls here. There they were, poor and alone, no one to take care of them, either grandmother or sister.

"She must have died soon after the children were born. For when I went in the morning to look after my neighbor, as soon as I entered the cottage, I found the poor thing dead and cold. And when she died she must have rolled over on this little girl . . . That's the way she crushed it, and spoiled this foot.

"The people got together, they washed and laid out the body, they had a coffin made, and buried her. The people were always kind. But the two little ones were left alone. What was to be done with them? Now I was the only one of the women who had a baby. For eight weeks I had been nursing my first-born.

a boy. So I took them for the time being. The peasants got together; they planned and planned what to do with them, and they said to me: —

"'You, Márya, just keep the little girls for a while, and give us a chance to decide.'"

"So I nursed the well one, but did not think it worth while to nurse the deformed one. I did not expect that she was going to live. And, then, I thought to myself, why should the little angel's soul pass away? and I felt sorry for it. I tried to nurse her, and so I had my own and these two besides; yes, I had three children at the breast. But I was young and strong, and I had good food! And God gave me so much milk in my breasts that I had enough and to spare. I used to nurse two at once and let the third one wait. When one was through, I would take up the third. And so God let me nurse all three; but when my boy was in his third year, I lost him. And God never gave me any more children. But we began to make money. And now we are living with the merchant at the mill. We get good wages and live well. But no children.

And how lonely it would be, if it were not for these two little girls! How could I help loving them? They are to me like the wax in the candle!"

And the woman pressed the little lame girl to her with one arm, and with the other hand she tried to wipe the tears from her cheeks.

And Matrióna sighed, and said: "The old saw isn't far wrong, 'Men can live without father and mother, but without God one cannot live.'"

While they were thus talking together suddenly a flash of lightning seemed to irradiate from that corner of the cottage where Mikháïla was sitting. All look at him; and behold! Mikháïla is sitting there with his hands folded in his lap, and looking up and smiling.

IX.

The woman went away with the children, and Mikháïla arose from the bench and laid down his work; he took off his apron, made a low bow to the shoemaker and his wife, and said:—

"Farewell, friends; God has forgiven me. Do you also forgive me?"

And Semyón and Matrióna perceived that it was from Mikháïla that the light had flashed. And Semyón arose, bowed low before Mikháïla, and said to him:—

"I see, Mikháïla, that you are not a mere man, and I have no right to detain you nor to ask questions of you. But tell me one thing: when I had found you and brought you home, you were sad; but when my wife gave you something to eat, you smiled upon her, and after that you became more cheerful. And then when the bárin ordered the boots, why did you smile a second time, and after that become still more cheerful; and now when this woman brought these two little girls, why did you smile for the third time and become radiant? Tell me, Mikháïla, why was it that such a light streamed from you, and why you smiled three times?"

And Mikháïla said:—

"The light blazed from me because I had been punished, but now God has forgiven me. And I smiled the three times because it was required of me to learn three of God's truths, and I have now learned the three truths of God. One truth I learned when your wife had pity on me, and so I smiled; the second truth I learned when the rich man ordered the boots, and I smiled for the second time; and now that I have seen the little girls, I have learned the third and last truth, and I smiled for the third time."

And Semyón said: —

"Tell me, Mikháila, why God punished you, and what were the truths of God, that I, too, may know them."

And Mikháila said: —

"God punished me because I disobeyed Him. I was an angel in heaven, and I was disobedient to God. I was an angel in heaven, and the Lord sent me to require a woman's soul. I flew down to earth; I see the woman lying alone — she is sick — she has just borne twins, two little girls. The little ones are sprawling about near their mother, but their mother is unable to lift them to her breast. The mother saw me; she perceived that God had sent me after her soul; she burst into tears, and said: —

"'Angel of God, I have just buried my husband; a tree fell on him in the forest and killed him. I have no sister, nor aunt, nor mother to take care of my little ones; do not carry off my soul*; let me bring up my children myself, and nurse them and put them on their feet. It is impossible for children to live without father or mother.'

"And I heeded what the mother said; I put one child to her breast, and laid the other in its mother's arms, and I returned to the Lord in heaven. I flew back to the Lord, and I said:—

"'I cannot take the mother's soul. The father has been killed by a tree, the mother has given birth to twins, and begs me not to take her soul; she says:—

"'"Let me bring up my little ones; let me nurse them and put them on their feet. It is impossible for children to live without father and mother." I did not take the mother's soul.'

"And the Lord said:—

"'Go and take the mother's soul, and thou

* *Dúshenka*, little soul, in the original.

shalt learn three lessons: Thou shalt learn *what is in men*, and *what is not given unto men*, and *what men live by*. When thou shalt have learned these three lessons, then return to heaven.'

"And I flew down to earth and took the mother's soul. The little ones fell from her bosom. The dead body rolled over on the bed, fell upon one of the little girls and crushed her foot. I rose above the village and was going to give the soul to God, when a wind seized me, my wings ceased to move and fell off, and the soul arose alone to God, and I fell back to earth."

X.

And Semyón and Matrióna now knew whom they had clothed and fed, and who it was that had been living with them, and they burst into tears of dismay and joy; and the angel said:—

"I was there in the field naked, and alone. Hitherto I had never known what human poverty was; I had known neither cold nor hunger, and now I was a man. I was famished, I was freezing, and I knew not what to do. And I saw across the field a chapel made for God's service. I went to God's chápel, thinking to get shelter in it. But the chapel was locked, and I could not enter. And I crouched down behind the chapel, so as to get shelter from the wind. Evening came; I was hungry and chill, and ached all over. Suddenly I hear a man walking along the road, with a pair of boots in his hand, and talking to himself. I now saw for the first time since I had become a man the face of a human being, and this man's face was deathly, and it filled me with dismay, and I tried to hide from him. And I heard this man asking himself how he should protect himself from cold during the winter, and how get food for his wife and children. And I thought:—

"'I am perishing with cold and hunger, and here is a man whose sole thought is to get a shuba for himself and his wife and to furnish bread for their sustenance. It is impossible for him to help me.'

"The man saw me and scowled; he seemed even more terrible than before; then he passed on. And I was in despair. Suddenly I heard the man coming back. I looked up, and did not recognize that it was the same man as before: then there was death in his face, but now it had suddenly become alive, and I saw that God was in his face. He came to me, put clothes upon me, and took me home with him.

"When I reached his house, a woman came out to meet us, and she began to scold. The woman was even more terrible to me than the man: a dead soul seemed to proceed forth from her mouth, and I was suffocated by the breath of death. She wanted to drive me out into the cold, and I knew that she would die if she drove me out. And suddenly her husband reminded her of God. And instantly a change came over the woman. And when she had prepared something for me to eat, and looked kindly upon me, I looked at her, and there was no longer anything like death about her; she was now alive, and in her also I recognized God.

"And I remembered God's first lesson: '*Thou shalt learn what is in men.*'

"And I perceived that LOVE was in men. And I was glad because God had begun to fulfil His promise to me, and I smiled for the first time. But I was not yet ready to know the whole. I could not understand what was not given to men, and what men live by.

"I began to live in your house, and after I had lived with you a year the man came to order the boots which should be strong enough to last him a year without ripping or wearing out of shape. And I looked at him, and suddenly perceived behind his back my comrade, the Angel of Death. No one besides myself saw this angel; but I knew him, and I knew that before the sun should go down, he would take the rich man's soul. And I said to myself: 'This man is laying his plans to live another year, and he knoweth not that ere evening comes he will be dead.'

"And I realized suddenly the second saying of God: '*Thou shalt know what is not given unto men.*'

"And now I knew what was in men. And now I knew also what was not given unto men. It is not given unto men to know what is needed for their bodies. And I smiled for the second time. I was glad because I saw my comrade, the angel, and because God had revealed unto me the second truth.

"But I could not yet understand all. I could not understand what men live by, and so I lived on, and waited until God should reveal to me the third truth also. And now in the sixth year the little twin girls have come with the woman, and I recognized the little ones, and I remembered how they had been left. And after I had recognized them, I thought:—

"'The mother besought me in behalf of her children, because she thought that it would be impossible for children to live without father and mother, but a stranger nursed them and brought them up.'

"And when the woman caressed the children that were not her own, and wept over them, then I saw in her THE LIVING GOD, and knew *what people live by*. And I knew that God had revealed to me the last truth, and had pardoned me, and I smiled for the last time."

XI.

And the angel's body became manifest, and he was clad with light so bright that the eyes could not endure to look upon him, and he spoke in clearer accents, as though the voice proceeded not from him, but came from heaven.

And the angel said: —

"I have learned that every man lives not through care of himself, but by love.

"It was not given to the mother to know what her children needed to keep them alive. It was not given the rich man to know what he himself needed, and it is not given to any man to know whether he will need boots for daily living, or slippers for his burial.

"When I became a man, I was kept alive, not by what thought I took for myself, but because a stranger and his wife had love in their hearts, and pitied and loved me. The orphans were kept alive, not because other people deliberated about what was to be done with them, but because a strange woman had love for them in her heart, and pitied them and loved them. And all men are kept alive, not by their own forethought, but because there is LOVE IN MEN.

"I knew before that God gave life to men, and desired them to live; but now I know something above and beyond that.

"I have learned that God does not wish men to live each for himself, and therefore He has not revealed to them what they each need for themselves, but He wishes them to live in union, and therefore He has revealed to them what is necessary for each and for all together.

"I have now learned that it is only in appearance that they are kept alive through care for themselves, but that in reality they are kept alive through love. *He who dwelleth in love dwelleth in God, and God in him, for God is love.*"

And the angel sang a hymn of praise to God, and the cottage shook with the sound of his voice.

And the ceiling parted, and a column of fire reached from earth to heaven. And Semyón and his wife and children fell prostrate on the ground. And pinions appeared upon the angel's shoulders, and he soared away to heaven.

And when Semyón opened his eyes, the cottage was the same as it had ever been, and there was no one in it save himself and his family.

WHAT IS WORTH WHILE SERIES.

AFTER COLLEGE, WHAT? For Girls. By Mrs. Helen E. Starrett.
ART OF LIVING (THE). By F. Emory Lyon.
BLESSING OF CHEERFULNESS. J. R. Miller, D.D.
BY THE STILL WATERS. By Rev. J. R. Miller, D.D.
CHILDREN'S WING (THE). By Elizabeth Glover.
CHRIST-FILLED LIFE (THE). By C. C. Hall, D.D.
CHRISTIAN'S ASPIRATIONS. By Rev.G.H.C.Macgregor.
CONFLICTING DUTIES. By E. S. Elliott.
CULTURE AND REFORM. By Anna R. Brown, Ph.D.
DO WE BELIEVE IT? By E. S. Elliott.
EXPECTATION CORNER. By E. S. Elliott.
FAMILY MANNERS. By Elizabeth Glover.
GENTLE HEART (A). By the Rev. J. R. Miller, D.D.
GIRLS: Faults and Ideals. By Rev. J. R. Miller, D.D.
GIVING WHAT WE HAVE. By Anna R. Brown, Ph.D.
GOLDEN RULE IN BUSINESS. By Rev. C. F. Dole.
HAPPY LIFE (THE). By Charles W. Eliott, LL.D.
HEAVENLY RECOGNITION. T. DeWitt Talmage, D.D.
J. COLE. By Emma Gellibrand.
JESSICA'S FIRST PRAYER. By Hesba Stretton.
KING OF THE GOLDEN RIVER. By John Ruskin.
LADDIE. By the author of "Miss Toosey's Mission."
LOVE AND FRIENDSHIP. By Ralph Waldo Emerson.
MASTER AND MAN. By Count Tolstoï.
MISS TOOSEY'S MISSION. By the author of "Laddie."
OF INTERCOURSE WITH GOD. Intro.by Rev.A.Murray.
PATHS OF DUTY (THE). By Dean Farrar.
REAL HAPPENINGS. By Mrs. Mary B. Claflin.
SECRETS OF HAPPY HOME LIFE. J. R. Miller, D.D.
SELF-CULTURE. By Wm. E. Channing, D.D.
SHIPS AND HAVENS. By Rev. Henry Van Dyke, D.D.
SOUL'S QUEST AFTER GOD. Rev. Lyman Abbott, D.D.
STILLNESS AND SERVICE. By E. S. Elliott.
SWEETNESS AND LIGHT. By Matthew Arnold.
TALKS ABOUT A FINE ART. By Elizabeth Glover.
TELL JESUS. By Anna Shipton.
TOO GOOD TO BE TRUE. By E. S. Elliott.
TRUE WOMANHOOD. By W. Cunningham, D.D.
TWO PILGRIMS (THE). By Count Lyof N. Tolstoï.
VICTORY OF OUR FAITH. By Anna R. Brown, Ph.D.
WHAT IS WORTH WHILE? By Anna R. Brown, Ph.D.
WHAT MEN LIVE BY. By Count Lyof N. Tolstoï.
WHEN THE KING COMES TO HIS OWN. Elliott.
WHEREFORE, O GOD? By the Rev. C. B. Herbert.
WHERE LOVE IS, THERE GOD IS ALSO. By L. N. Tolstoï.
YOUNG MEN: Faults and Ideals. Rev. J. R. Miller, D.D.

For sale by all booksellers, or sent, postpaid, by the publishers, on receipt of 35c.

THOMAS Y. CROWELL & CO., NEW YORK & BOSTON.

Lightning Source UK Ltd.
Milton Keynes UK
UKHW021520170619
344552UK00005B/1252/P